Mungo Monkey
has a Birthday Party

Lydia Monks

EGMONT

This is Mungo.

It's his birthday tomorrow!

All of Mungo's friends
are invited to his party.

Morning!

On the day of the party . . .

Mungo has lots to do before the party . . .

makes party hats

Oops!

Mungo wakes up very early!

Which party outfit will Mungo pick?

What a lot of presents!
Which one would you like?

Mungo and his friends play
Pass the Parcel

and Musical Statues.

Now it's time for Mungo to blow out his candles and make a wish.

Mungo wished for
a sleepover with
his friends!

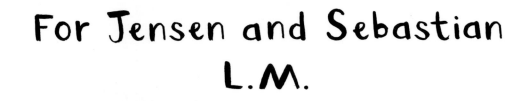

For Jensen and Sebastian
L.M.

EGMONT
We bring stories to life

First published in Great Britain 2014
by Egmont UK Limited
The Yellow Building, 1 Nicholas Road, London W11 4AN
www.egmont.co.uk

Text and illustrations copyright © Lydia Monks 2014
Lydia Monks has asserted her moral rights.

ISBN 978 1 4052 6866 0

Stay safe online. Any website addresses listed in this book are correct at the
time of going to print. However, Egmont is not responsible for content hosted
by third parties. Please be aware that online content can be subject to
change and websites can contain content that is unsuitable for children.
We advise that all children are supervised when using the internet.

FSC
www.fsc.org
MIX
Paper from
responsible sources
FSC® C018306